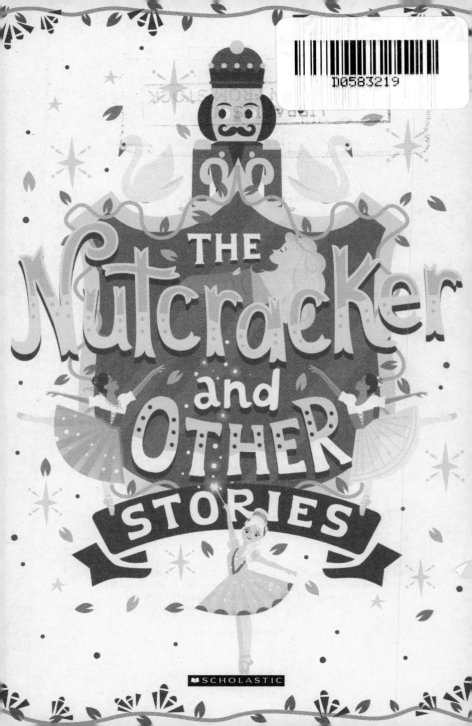

THE Nutcracker and OTHER STORIES

■SCHOLASTIC

Scholastic Children's Books
An imprint of Scholastic Ltd
Euston House, 24 Eversholt Street, London, NW1 1DB, UK
Registered office: Westfield Road, Southam, Warwickshire, CV47 0RA
SCHOLASTIC and associated logos are trademarks and/or
registered trademarks of Scholastic Inc.

First published in the UK by Scholastic Ltd, 2018

Text copyright © Emma Adams 2018
Illustrations copyright © Risa Rodil 2018

The moral rights of Emma Adams and Risa Rodil to be identified as
the author and illustrator of this work have been asserted.

ISBN 978 1407 19145 4

A CIP catalogue record for this book
is available from the British Library.

The publisher does not have any control over and does not assume responsibility
for the illustrator or third-party websites of their content.

Printed and bound by CPI Group (UK) Ltd, Croydon, CR0 4YY

Papers used by Scholastic Children's Books are made from wood grown in
sustainable forests.

3 5 7 9 10 8 6 4 2

www.scholastic.co.uk

For my mum,
Thank you for never making me wear pink,
and thank you for letting me be exactly how I
wanted to be. You helped a weird little girl grow
up into a very happy (and still weird) woman.

Contents

Introduction

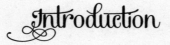

The origins of ballet can be dated back to fifteenth-century Italy, when dances and masked balls became popular in the courts of the Italian Renaissance. Later, when Catherine de Medici of Italy married King Henry II of France in 1533, Italian dance was introduced to the French court. From there, both France and Russia developed their own styles of ballet, and by 1850 Russia in particular had built itself a reputation as one of the leading creative entities for ballet at that time. Over the years, stylistic variations emerged and different styles of ballet developed, including classical, romantic, neoclassical and contemporary. Russian Prima Ballerina Anna Pavlovna; founder of Harlem's Dance Theatre, American Arthur Mitchell; Prima Ballerina and choreographer Natalia Makarova; and Latvian and American dancer, choreographer and actor Mikhail Nikolayevich Baryshnikov are just some of the dancers who became famous in the world of ballet in the twenty-first century.

Swan Lake

Composed by Pyotr Ilyich Tchaikovsky, "Swan Lake" was likely inspired by Russian and German folk tales, such as "The White Duck" and "The Stolen Veil". There is no evidence to indicate who wrote the original libretto. Some believe it was the prolific Czechoslovakian choreographer Julius Reisinger, while others say it was Russian dramatist Vladimir Petrovich Begichev. Whoever it was, the ballet premiered at the Bolshoi Theatre in Moscow on the 20th February 1877, but was not well received. It has stood the test of time, however, and is now one of the most popular of all ballets.

In the glittering daylight, on a gloriously warm summer's day, a bustle of excitement was in the air. It was His Royal Highness Prince Siegfried's birthday, and that evening a grand celebration would take place to mark the event. Royal staff cheerfully hung garlands of flowers in the palace courtyard while talking and laughing. Oh, there was much excitement!

As the day wore on, the merriment continued, and at last dusk started to fall and the party was ready to begin.

When Prince Siegfried entered the courtyard, there were cheers from all around. Many people had travelled far and wide to be present at his coming-of-age ceremony, and they crowded into the palace in their vast number. At the centre of it all, Prince Siegfried stood, and so happy was he. It was his name day, after all, and as you can imagine he enjoyed all the privileges that any young prince could hope for. So used to being free and without responsibility was the prince, that he was much taken aback when his mother came to speak with him about something very specific during the party.

"My dear son," she said, "you are now of age, and you must surely know what that means?" Of course, the prince did indeed know what his mother was alluding to, but he had not been expecting her to discuss such things with him at a public event. "Mother, please," he sighed, and he suddenly felt weary. "Must we talk about this now?" But his mother persisted. He had come of age, she repeated, and so he must find a wife. It was his duty to his country.

As a young man – and especially as a young man of royalty – Prince Siegfried was used to doing exactly as he pleased, and so the conversation with his mother was received with shock. *I am but twenty-one years old*, he thought, *and I am to marry*? All at once, the responsibility of his role started to feel real. To avoid his mother, and perhaps so that he could distract himself from what he had just learned, Prince Siegfried banded together his closest friends for a spot of hunting. Armed with their crossbows, they stalked towards the forest as the day grew dark.

On their way, the prince spotted a flock of swans flying above their heads, regal and in a beautiful v-formation. "What do you think?" the prince asked his friends. "Shall I make the head swan my prey?" Flying quickly as they were, the swans were already far ahead of the group, and so it was with much effort that Prince Siegfried tried to catch up to them. Into the forest he crashed, running in the direction he had perceived the swans to be flying. Looking upwards through the trees ahead of him, he continued to keep the swans in his sight, until suddenly they seemed to disappear. Not wishing to be beaten, the prince continued, and after just a moment more he found himself within a beautiful clearing. Light shone through the canopy of trees above and sparkled across the water of a large lake in front of which he stood. There was something in the air – something that told the prince that this was an unusual place. The clearing, and all within it, felt … magical. *Is this lake enchanted?* he wondered, as he started to walk around it. He was soon to find out, for, just ahead of him he now spotted the swans. There were seven of them and they were truly the most beautiful specimens he had come across. Now, instead of raising his crossbow to them, the prince only felt relief at the fact that he hadn't taken aim before; at a distance, he had not known how majestic and magnificent these creatures were, but now that he stood before them he had no desire to threaten their lives.

The swans, sensing that the prince no longer wished to harm them, swam towards him and with surprise he saw that the most striking swan – the one leading the others – was wearing a crown. "How entirely curious," Prince Siegfried said aloud, his confusion overwhelming him.

He was aware that the day was growing darker and darker still while he stood there, watching the swans drift slowly across the glistening waters. There was less light filtering through the trees above them. But somehow the lake appeared illuminated, as if some light were shining from within it. As night finally fell, Prince Siegfried found himself holding his breath for some unknown reason. It was as if he were waiting for something to happen, such was the stillness in the air around him. And it wasn't long before something did indeed happen: as the prince continued to watch the swans, he saw their leader break away from the others and swim towards the bank of the lake. Mesmerized, the prince continued to watch, and was stunned to see that as the swan approached the bank and emerged from the water, it was transformed into a beautiful young lady.

Strangely, Prince Siegfried did not feel fear, although he realized that perhaps he should, as he did not know the woman who stood before him and for all he knew she could be a witch. In hushed tones, he asked her as much. She smiled at him, though it was a sad smile.

"I am no witch," she said. "If I were, then perhaps I wouldn't find myself enchanted so. You see, my name is Odette and I am a princess. A sorcerer called Von Rothbart – a truly spiteful man – once asked me to marry him. When I said no, because I did not love him, he cursed me and my maids in waiting, committing us to the life we now live. When the sun is in the sky," she continued, "we are swans. But when night falls, our natural forms return to us."

Prince Siegfried was moved to tears upon hearing Princess Odette's words, and he wished in earnest that there were something he could do. "Can the enchantment be broken?" he asked, looking deep into her eyes. "Only if a person, pure in heart, pledges their love to me and does not betray me," said the princess. Her eyes told the prince that she had lost all hope of this happening, but, seeing her standing there, in the soft glow of the moonlight and the evanescent light that came from the lake, Prince Siegfried knew in his heart what he wanted to do. "I will be that person," he said, strongly. "I pledge my love to you, and I will not betray you, Odette." With that, Siegfried and Odette embraced each other, and it felt as if this was not their first meeting – it was as if they already knew each other. Their embrace turned into the most beautiful dance, as their arms weaved together and their bodies entwined. Siegfried stayed until the early hours, and until the sun threatened to rise into the sky, committing Odette to her unnatural swan form once more.

The next evening, Prince Siegfried was summoned to the great hall. He pulled at his collar, feeling ill at ease in his clothes after having been told to dress in formal attire. "What do my parents have in store for me now?" he wondered aloud as he walked across the stone entranceway that lay before the great hall. He was soon to find out. "Prince Siegfried!" announced the royal herald as the heavy doors to the hall were opened for him, and with a sinking stomach the prince saw that a feast was well under way. This was obviously of his parents' doing, so determined were they to match him with a suitor.

Not wanting to offend his guests, Prince Siegfried tried his best to hide his obvious displeasure. However, he found it hard to keep a level temper with his parents, next to whom he sat during the feast.

"Just look at all of these wonderful suitors!" said his father. "Does not even one of them appeal to you, my son?" His mother was equally enthusiastic. "Why, there are so many beauties within this room!" she observed. "And if you picked one of them, you would make your father and I so happy."

Though he had no doubt that the people his parents had brought to the hall were indeed most worthy of his attentions, he could not stop thinking about Odette. His heart broke for her, stuck as she was in her enchanted prison, and he wanted to break the curse so that she could return to being a human again and they could be together. All he needed was to marry Odette. After that, he would have all the time in the world to explain to his parents.

But as his parents continued to press him,

the prince started to feel very tired indeed. *Perhaps I should agree to dance with one or two of the guests*, he thought, *if not for anything else, it would allow me some respite from my tiresome parents.*

And so, dance he did – with as much merriment as he could muster. During the prince's second dance, the royal trumpets were blown to signal the arrival of another guest, but the prince didn't catch their name, so loud was the music. Glancing to the entranceway, Siegfried was astonished to see Odette, wearing the most beautiful attire and a crown that sparkled in the evening light. "How is this so?" he said aloud, forgetting himself completely.

Quickly excusing himself from the dance, he walked quickly across the great hall and was at Odette's side within a moment. "I don't understand," he said, "how is it that you are here?" he looked at her searchingly, but Odette only smiled and blushed. Prince Siegfried became aware of a man beside her. "Please," he said, "won't you dance with my daughter? She has so been looking forward to this moment." Prince Siegfried agreed most willingly, and though this dance with Odette felt different from the one they had shared upon the bank of the lake, he tried not to dwell on it. *Perhaps it is merely because we are surrounded by so many people*, he thought.

Prince Siegfried and Odette spent many hours in each other's arms that evening, and it wasn't until the festivities were about to end that they sat down for a rest. "I still cannot believe that it's you," said Siegfried. "This evening had been truly magical, and I don't want it to end. It mustn't end." He looked at Odette with tears in his eyes and smiled. "Odette, will you marry me?"

In that moment, the prince caught sight of something out of the corner of his eye – movement just outside the window that was closest to them – and with shock, he was certain he saw Odette fleeing from the palace grounds. Looking back to the woman who sat in front of him, he was dismayed to see that, while she looked similar to Odette, she was not in fact his love. She smiled at him cruelly. "Meet my father," she said, as the man who had first introduced them approached, "Von Rothbart." Prince Siegfried recoiled in horror and stumbled away from them. The evening had simply been a way for Von Rothbart to exact further revenge upon Odette, by enchanting his daughter to look like her and thus tricking Siegfried in the most terrible of ways.

As he ran into the night, Siegfried was

filled with regret. He had known that something felt strange when he had danced with the woman who looked like Odette, but he had wanted to believe that it was her. Now he had no chance of breaking Odette's enchantment, for he had betrayed her. When he arrived at the lake, Siegfried found Odette surrounded by swans. Though at first she did not want to speak with him, she granted Siegfried a few moments to explain himself, and as he relayed the truth about the evening and Von Rothbart's involvement, he and Odette were both overcome with sadness. "Please forgive me, Odette," he said, for he feared his heart would break if she did not. Odette looked into his eyes. "I do forgive you," she said, even though her own heart was itself broken.

But their moment of peace would not last long, for Von Rothbart and his daughter were also on their way to the lake. Seeing Odette and Siegfried entwined in an embrace, Von Rothbart called out to him on his arrival. "Get away from her!" he shrieked. "Get away! You betrayed her when you promised yourself to my daughter – and that promise must stand. You must marry my daughter!"

"I would rather die!" said Prince Siegfried defiantly, and in that moment he felt sure that this was true. As he and Odette looked into each other's eyes, an unspoken agreement passed between them. They knew what they must do. Taking each other's hand, they began their descent into the lake. "Stop," shouted Von Rothbart, "stop!" But they would not, and with every step their grip upon each other tightened. As they disappeared into the lake, the sorcerer screamed with anger. And then something unexpected happened: the swans, who were Odette's ladies in waiting, were transformed back into humans. Because of Odette's death, the enchantment was finally broken. As Von Rothbart and his daughter fled, the ladies in waiting stood by the lakeside in sorrow. But while they looked out across the water, they saw two shimmering auras rising from the water. As the auras ascended, each lady in waiting felt enveloped by a sense of calm, for now they knew that, in death, Odette and Siegfried could finally be together.

Coppélia

The Girl with the Enamel Eyes

Originally choreographed by Arthur Saint-Léon to music composed by Léo Delibes, Coppélia is a comic ballet based on two stories by ETA Hoffmann: "The Sandman" ("Der Sandmann") and "The Doll" ("Die Puppe").

In a small town, on a warm and sunny day, the townsfolk were in the midst of preparing for a wonderful celebration. You see, the town had been gifted with a new bell, and the bell was to arrive that very day. People rushed this way and that, doing what they could ahead of the bell's arrival. One of those people was Franz, a young man who had grown up in the village and was engaged to a young woman called Swanhilda. Franz loved Swanhilda very much, but recently he had found his head turned by a lady who he saw on the balcony of Doctor Coppélius, who was well-known in the town as being an inventor and a rather eccentric man. The woman was known to be his daughter, but she never left the house.

It was one afternoon many days before that Franz had first seen the woman. Dressed in beautiful clothing, she sat upon a delicate chair on the balcony and read silently. Franz had only seen her upon the balcony, and he had only seen her reading – he never saw her in the village, and she did not seem to participate in other activities, even within the confines of her home. *How strange it is that she spends all of her time up there*, thought Franz. Because he had never had a conversation with the mysterious woman, he started to become quite infatuated with her and imagined a great many things about her without even knowing if they were true. *She looks very studious*, he thought, *and I'm sure she is both courteous and kind*. Before long, Franz found out that the woman's name was Coppélia.

Swanhilda, to whom Franz was of course

engaged, had noticed something different about him and her suspicions were that it was because of Coppélia. Swanhilda knew Coppélia to be beautiful, for she had seen her beauty with her own eyes, and she felt very upset with Franz for his transfer of affections. *How could he?* thought Swanhilda to herself, feeling that Franz had betrayed her.

After noticing that Franz had grown more and more distant, Swanhilda resolved to visit Coppélia. She would find out if a bond was growing between the two, she decided. She gathered some of her closest friends and they made their way to Doctor Coppélius' household, being sure to stay hidden as they did so, for they did not want the doctor himself to know what they were doing. They stopped not far from the doctor's front door and waited. It was not long before the doctor emerged, leaving for the day to run errands of some sort, and with interest Swanhilda saw that the doctor accidentally dropped his key as he walked away. After retrieving the key, Swanhilda allowed entry to the house for her and her friends, although some of them really didn't want to go.

"What if he comes back?" they said. "He will surely be angry." But Swanhilda did not listen, such was her determination to find Coppélia. As they made their way through the house, the young women were struck by the silence there. It was so quiet that you would surely hear a pin if it dropped, and the silence held an eeriness. After opening the doors to a series of rooms but finding nothing of interest, Swanhilda finally approached the last room in the house. With a deep breath, she turned the handle, and through the doorway each of them walked.

To their surprise, the room was filled with people. Their first instinct was to turn and run, for they would only get in trouble if they were seen, but very quickly Swanhilda realized that there was something unusual about the people within the room. For, aside from she herself and her friends, none of the people were actually moving. As they walked amongst the figures that were frozen in place, they realized what they were: life-sized dolls. Finding large mechanisms in their backs, the women wound up each doll and the room burst into motion as the dolls moved in the ways their mechanics allowed. Drawn to a curtain, Swanhilda pulled it aside and gasped. It was Coppélia. She too was a mechanical doll. Suddenly the women felt quite afraid, for what sort of inventor created false people as these? But to their terror, they heard a noise elsewhere in the house: Doctor Coppélius had returned.

Having realized that someone had entered his house uninvited, the doctor immediately made his way to the room containing his dolls and was outraged to find the women within it. In anger, he shouted at them to leave, and so terrified were they that they did so immediately. But while the doctor made sure that the door was locked behind them, someone else had made their way into the doctor's house: Franz.

Just like Swanhilda, Franz had wished to speak with Coppélia, and having seen the doctor in the town, Franz had rushed to the doctor's house. But upon knocking on the door he found that no one answered. *How strange*, he thought, before a new thought occurred to him: *could Coppélia be in trouble?* Resolving to climb up to her balcony, Franz scaled the walls of the doctor's house and peered through the window. It was in this moment that he came face-to-face with Doctor Coppélius himself.

Having gone back to the room to set straight the mess that the women had made in his absence, Doctor Coppélius had only just started to rearrange the dolls when he noticed a presence at the window. It was Franz, of course, but instead of wishing him away, as he had done with Swanhilda and her friends, the doctor was suddenly struck by a gruesome idea. You see, Doctor Coppélius did not want his inventions to stay as dolls. He wanted to evoke a magic spell that he believed would bring his dolls to life. In this way, the doctor was sadly a very delusional man, and now he was about to become very dangerous indeed, as he believed that, for his magic spell to work, he needed a human sacrifice. So when he saw Franz at his window, and realized that no one else knew about Franz's whereabouts, he made his decision to sacrifice Franz.

Doctor Coppélius welcomed Franz in, and so unsuspecting was he that he gladly entered. "Doctor Coppélius, sir," said Franz, "please accept my apologies for arriving here in such an unusual fashion. I stopped by to see Coppélia and was alarmed when she did not answer the door. I thought," he added, "that she might be in danger."

"Come in, my dear boy, come in," said the doctor, doing his best to sound jovial. Inside the doctor's house, Franz had made himself comfortable on one of the doctor's chairs. "Coppélia is quite well, I can assure you," said the doctor, "in fact, she is out herself — but due back any moment," he added quickly, as he did not want Franz to leave. "Here, won't you take a drink with me?" Franz happily accepted, and, realizing how parched he felt, drank the drink he had been given very quickly indeed. No sooner had he sipped the last drop but did Franz start to feel sleepy, and too late he realized that the doctor must have placed something in his drink to send him to sleep. In confusion he fell into an odd slumber.

All of this had happened because the doctor thought they were alone in the room, but in fact this was not true, for Swanhilda, who had been behind the curtain when the doctor returned home, was still hiding there out of sight. From her vantage point, Swanhilda had heard everything, and she felt extremely fearful for Franz. As quickly and silently as she could, Swanhilda dressed herself in Coppélia's clothes. As she emerged from behind the curtain, the doctor was overjoyed. His magic spell had worked, or so he believed for here was his beloved Coppélia standing alive before him! While he was distracted by his own rejoicing, Swanhilda woke Franz from his stupor. Such was his disorientation that, at first, he too thought Swanhilda was Coppélia. When Franz came to he realized that it was in fact Swanhilda who stood before him, and as she wound up the mechanical dolls that surrounded them Franz realized the error of his ways. Oh, how silly he had been! In the commotion, they were able to escape, but not before Doctor Coppélius tried his best to stop them. "Coppélia!" he cried, "Coppélia! Come back to me!" But in his confusion he pulled on the curtain behind which Swanhilda had been hiding and saw, to his great dismay, the real Coppélia. He had not brought her to life after all.

Only once they were safely back in the town did Swanhilda and Franz dare to stop and catch their breath. They had both come close to death, they realized, and the thought of losing one another was almost too much to bear. With their love renewed, they decided to uphold their engagement despite Franz's transgression, for everything they had been through had made them stronger.

Sleeping Beauty

Known as "La Belle au Bois Dormant" (Sleeping Beauty) in French, "DornröschenI" (Little Briar Rose) in German and "The Sleeping Beauty in the Woods" in English, this classic fairy tale was originally written by Charles Perrault. Ivan Vsevolozhsky's ballet, based on Perrault's tale, was scored by Russian Composer Pyotr Ilyich Tchaikovsky. First performed at the Mariinsky Theatre in St Petersburg on 15th January 1890, "Sleeping Beauty" went on to become one of the most famous classical ballets in history.

There was once a king and queen who very much wanted a child. Time passed but no child was born unto them, which made them terribly sad. Still, they dared to hope that one day their dream would come true and, indeed, after much waiting, the king and queen finally had a baby girl. For this they were filled with joy.

A great celebration was arranged and relatives, friends and all acquaintances were invited to share the king and queen's happiness. As well as this, the king invited the fairies of the realm, of which there were seven. The king and queen planned to ask the fairies to be godmothers to their dear child, and as such they fashioned seven gold trinkets – one for each fairy – to bestow as a gift.

The feast was a celebration like nothing the kingdom had ever seen before, with much merriment, dancing and singing. And before long the fairies rose and surrounded the new princess, for each fairy had chosen to bestow their own gift upon her. The first fairy chose kindness, the second chose intelligence, the third chose curiosity, the fourth chose strength, the fifth chose resilience and the sixth chose determination. But when the time came for the seventh fairy to speak, a commotion broke out in the grand hall as an eighth fairy stormed in. She had not been invited, and she was furious. The king and queen professed their apologies at their mistake; they didn't realize that she would want to attend, they explained, as she had not left her tower for many, many years. "Please," begged the king, "forgive us this oversight — we did not mean it as an insult." But it was no good. The fairy, much angered by them and wanting revenge, made a declaration to all in witness.

"The princess shall indeed grow to possess all of the gifts that my sisters have bestowed upon her," she said, her voice raised high so all could hear. "But in her fifteenth year, she shall prick her hand on a spindle and die!"

Gasps of horror spread across the hall, and the king and queen's were surely the loudest. The fairy left the hall as chaos engulfed the crowds of people around her. The king and queen were terribly distraught, such was their love for the child they had waited so patiently to be born. And that was when the seventh fairy stepped forward. She could not undo the spell of the eighth, she said with sadness, but she would cast a spell so that if the princess pricked her finger she would be taken into a deep sleep instead.

The king, frightened by the possible death of his beloved child, decreed that all spindles across the land be burned immediately, and an enormous bonfire blazed within the castle grounds that very night, as the townsfolk joined together to burn every single spindle in existence. Or so they thought.

Years passed, and the princess grew into a fine young lady showing all of the virtues that the fairies had given her. For a while, all in the kingdom lived happily. They even forgot about the terrible prophecy the eighth fairy had delivered.

But on the day of the princess's fifteenth birthday, she awoke early with a start. Instead of going down to eat breakfast with her parents, she chose to explore the palace, and, upon doing so, she came across a staircase that she had never seen before. She climbed the stone steps and found a small room, with an old woman sitting inside, busily spinning flax at a spindle. So old was the woman that she rarely left the room, as her tired legs did not want to climb up and down so many steps. So she had not attended the princess's birthday celebrations all those years before and she did not know of the spiteful prediction the eighth fairy had made.

Seeing the spindle, but not knowing what it was, the princess was overcome with curiosity and reached out her hand to touch it. But as soon as she pricked her finger, the curse was fulfilled and she immediately fell into a deep sleep. As the princess fell to the floor in a magical slumber, the old woman, who was good and kind, cried for help.

The king and queen were devastated, but

were able to forgive the elderly woman, for they knew that what had happened was not done in malice. The princess was carried to a special room, where she could sleep in peace and safety; but to ensure that she would not be threatened further by the eighth fairy, the seventh fairy decided to cast a spell upon the entire kingdom. Sending the king and queen to their chambers, the seventh fairy set about casting the spell. The king and queen fell asleep in their chamber, townsfolk fell asleep in their cottages, horses fell asleep in their stalls, dogs fell asleep in the courtyard – even birds fell asleep in the trees. The fairy's spell spread across the land like a blanket, covering it in silence, while around the castle a terrible forest of thorns grew, so dense and dangerous that nothing could get through.

As the years passed, many forgot about the legend of the sleeping kingdom. The thorns covered it so completely that no one even knew it was there. But, one hundred years later, a prince came to the country and spied a tall tower above an enormous forest of thorns. "What is in the tower?" he asked people, "and how has such a dangerous forest come to grow around it?" The answers he received were many: some said the tower was part of an old, haunted castle; others said that witches occupied it. The prince heard that many had died trying to reach the tower; however, he was filled with determination: he would journey inside the thorny forest. But as the prince approached it, a curious thing occurred: the thorns parted for him, allowing him to pass through unharmed. It had been one hundred years exactly, you see, and the spell that created the thorns was now broken. Through the kingdom the prince walked, seeing people sleeping in every place — in the walkways, at tables, even on horses who were also asleep themselves. At first he thought them to be dead, and was horrified by the sight. But on closer inspection he saw them to be in the deepest of slumbers. Further and further he walked, until he came to the castle. Though he had never been there before, the prince was drawn to a staircase that contained many stone steps. Finally, he reached a door and upon opening it came to the room where the princess was sleeping.

So peaceful was she that at first the prince forgot himself. Kneeling down beside her, he looked at her face, so rested in sleep, and leaned down to kiss her hand. As soon as his lips touched her, the princess awoke.

They went downstairs together and saw that the kingdom was starting to wake too. The king and queen looked at one another in confusion, at first not knowing what had happened. As the prince told them, they listened in amazement and decided to celebrate with the kingdom once more. And so, that evening, and one hundred years late, the princess celebrated her fifteenth birthday with the prince by her side.

Giselle

The idea for the ballet version of "Giselle" came from French poet and novelist Théophile Gautier, who was inspired by German poet Heinrich Heine's retelling of a Slavic legend about ghostly female spirits. Gautier presented his idea to the Paris Opéra, and French composer Adolphe Adam was brought in to work on it. The ballet debuted in Paris on June 28th 1841.

In the picturesque village of Thurnigen, in Germany's Rhineland, lived a young girl called Giselle. Giselle was a peasant girl of low means, but she worked hard and was well thought of by many of the villagers. As it happened, Giselle was also very beautiful.

In Thurnigen, the villagers passed down tales and legends from generation to generation, strongly believing in the magic and mystery of tales told to them when they were but small children. There were parts of the forest, they knew, that were haunted by spirits still wandering on earth, and those wandering through woodland at night were often at risk of encountering such beings.

Of all of these legends, the one that seemed to capture the villagers' imaginations the most strongly was that of the Wilis. Said to reveal themselves only between the hours of midnight and four in the morning, the Wilis were known to be the ghostly spirits of young maidens who had been deceived and abandoned by their loves. These sorrowful spirits were often seen dancing together in a darkened glade in a far corner of the forest. It was said that their other-worldly figures would create the most beautiful formations, weaving to and fro together in an endless dance while the moon hung high in the sky.

For all of their beauty, though, the Wilis were known to be a danger to all men because of their own woeful histories. The pain they had been made to feel while alive stayed with them in death, and even turned into anger and the need to seek revenge. If any man found himself unlucky enough to come across a group of dancing Wilis under the cover of darkness, he would know deep in his heart that his end was near. For the Wilis would surround their prey in a circle of supernatural movement that made all and every man lose themselves to the dancing. Round and round they would spin, mirroring the mournful actions they saw before them. But when they felt tired, they were unable to stop. Such was the control held over them by the Wilis. On and on they would dance, until sheer exhaustion set in and they would fall to the ground dead.

And so, as you can quite imagine, no man would willingly wander the forest at night, for fear of what might become of them. Indeed, the women too were warned of the dancing Wilis, for it was believed that the women who came into contact with them in life had more chance of becoming one in death.

Giselle was a peasant girl who had grown up hearing many stories of the Wilis — perhaps more stories than most maidens were told, for Giselle loved to dance and often did so, which many villagers feared would make her more susceptible to the Wilis. Not only did Giselle love to dance, but she was very beautiful too, and as such there were two young men who hoped to gain her love. One was called Hilarion. Hilarion was a gamekeeper who lived on the outskirts of the forest. Giselle and Hilarion had known each other for many years and over this time he had fallen deeply in love with her. They often spent time together, but recently Hilarion had noticed Giselle withdrawing from him, and he suspected that she had met someone else. In this, Hilarion was right, because Giselle had indeed met someone — a kind young man called Loys. Giselle found Loys so charming that she very quickly started to fall in love with him, but there was a secret that he kept from her and it was a very large secret indeed. The truth was that Loys was in fact Albrecht, Duke of Silesia. As a duke, Albrecht was forced to marry whomever his parents decided, and so when he had met Giselle he did not want to admit his identity to her. Instead, he told her that he was a villager and he took up temporary residence in a small cottage occupied by his squire, Wilfred, to aid his deception. As a result, Albrecht found himself in an extremely complicated situation, for he was in fact betrothed to another – Princess Balthilde of Courland. The marriage was expected to take place at some point in the future, but Albrecht wished it would not. Still, you may be wondering why all of this meant he had to conceal his identity from Gisele? Albrecht knew that he would not be permitted by his parents to marry Giselle, for he was a duke and she was not of the same social standing as he. He knew that if Giselle found out his true identity, she would stop seeing him altogether, so he kept it a secret in order to keep seeing her.

Giselle and Loys met many times. They would discuss books, philosophy and other interesting things. And with each meeting their bond became stronger. At the village dances, Giselle danced more beautifully and more frequently than before, and was thrilled to learn that Loys was an excellent dancer himself. But Hilarion was of course far from happy about Giselle's growing affection for Loys. More than this, Hilarion felt that there was something distrustful about Loys, and he decided to keep close watch over him because of this. Another person who was unhappy about the relationship was Wilfred. Wilfred was filled with the fear that Albrecht's secret would be revealed, as it is well known by anyone that secrets always become uncovered in the end, and usually in some disastrous manner.

So it was not surprising that one morning, when Albrecht was preparing to meet Giselle, Wilfred once again tried in earnest to dissuade him. The deception was dangerous, he said, and would surely be revealed. And what about Giselle? Whenever the secret did come out, her feelings would be hurt in the most terrible way. But Albrecht would not listen. Instead, he became angry and ordered Wilfred to stop his interference. Later that morning, Albrecht set off for his meeting with Giselle feeling light of heart. As he saw her in the distance, he ran to her and swept her up into an embrace. However, the couple were being watched by another: Hilarion. He was of course suspicious of Loys and feared he could not be trusted. But whenever he had tried to express his concerns to Giselle, she would not listen, so blinded by devotion was she. Because of this, Hilarion decided to keep a watchful eye on Loys. If there was anything untruthful about the fellow, then he would soon find out.

As Hilarion watched Giselle and Loys, he became aware of villagers approaching in the distance. Crouching down further out of sight, he saw that the men and women were carrying large baskets of grapes and singing merrily. The grapes were to be made into wine, and the villagers were in good spirits thanks to the harvest celebrations they were preparing for. When the men and women saw Giselle and Loys dancing so merrily, they were swept into the dancing, setting aside their baskets and joining hands amongst themselves. There were shouts of joy and encouragement – indeed, the whole group was having a marvellous time – but in their excitement they had become very loud, and Giselle's mother Berthe, who lived but a stone's throw away, was led to them by the loud laughter. Seeing her daughter dancing in the arms of a young man troubled Berthe deeply. She too felt there was something amiss about Loys – something that could not be trusted – and she wished that Giselle would heed her concerns about him. But her worries were more deeply rooted than this. Berthe's health was extremely delicate, and so she had never been able to dance with the same abandon as her daughter. There was a chance, however, that Giselle could inherit the same ill health as her mother. If this ever came to be, the dancing she so enjoyed could damage her health permanently. Time and time again Berthe tried to warn her daughter, but time and time again she would not listen. So on this day, when Berthe saw Giselle ignoring her words once more, she was overcome with disappointment. Approaching her daughter, Berthe scolded Giselle for her carelessness. "Not only do you waste your time dancing," said Berthe, "but you threaten your health as well. What will become of you? You will be transformed into a Wilis if you continue to conduct yourself in such ways."

Giselle turned her mother away, but as she did so a party of noblemen and noblewomen appeared in the distance. Galloping on their horses, they had made their way to the village seeking refreshment after their long ride. With horror, Albrecht realized that his betrothed, Bathilde, was amongst the new arrivals. If Bathilde saw him, he would be exposed, so Albrecht snuck away to his small cottage in the woods and left Giselle to dance with the village folk. Not knowing the real reason for his disappearance, Giselle joined the other villagers in welcoming the newcomers, and soon enough everyone was dancing again with much revelry. Everyone, that is, except Wilfred, who had arrived on horseback with Bathilde. As he stood in the crowd between Giselle and Bathilde, Wilfred felt very anxious indeed, and it was only a matter of time before the two women came face-to-face. But they still knew nothing of each other, and Giselle curtsied before Princess Bathilde, as she was so in awe of her. In return, Bathilde found Giselle's sweetness endearing, and was so charmed that she offered Giselle her necklace as a gift before she departed with her group. As the noblemen and noblewomen set off, Albrecht finally came out of his hiding place, and rejoined Giselle and the villagers. He had managed to avoid being found out, but his relief would not last long, for when Albrecht had hidden himself away in the cottage, Hilarion had secretly followed him there and lay in wait until Albrecht made his way back to Giselle. Once the cottage lay empty, Hilarion took it upon himself to search through the belongings he found within. Low and behold, he came across something that was incriminating indeed.

Hilarion returned to the festivities in a blind rage, shouting so angrily that everyone stopped dancing at once. Approaching Albrecht and Giselle, he threw something down at their feet: Albrecht's sword. Made of silver and with a hilt of intricate design, the sword could only be owned by a nobleman, not a villager as Albrecht had pretended to be. "I found this in your cottage," he shouted, "along with fine clothes that only someone of wealth could own. You are not who you said you were. Admit it!" By now Hilarion was shrieking loudly, while shaking with anger. When Albrecht tried to refute the allegations, Hilarion blew loudly and clearly upon his hunting horn. Within moments, the sound of hooves could be heard as the party of noblemen and noblewomen returned. Bathilde spotted Albrecht immediately and ran to embrace him, and thus the duke's deceitful ways were revealed. The villagers were furious on behalf of their dear Giselle, and the noblemen and noblewomen were furious on behalf of their princess. But anger very quickly turned into sadness for Giselle, so heartbroken was she. Overcome with grief, she pulled from her neck the necklace that the princess had given her only a short while before and threw it to the ground, before closing her eyes. And as the people surrounding her looked on with worry, Giselle danced. She danced for the love she had felt for Albrecht but now knew to be based on a lie; she danced for her heart that had broken so surely that she felt it would never repair. She danced and danced, and the villagers and nobility alike were mesmerized by her. But in her final act of despair, Giselle, overcome from exhaustion and sadness, collapsed. Breathing her last breath, she died in Albrecht's arms as Berthe wept over her daughter's body.

Giselle was buried and a gravestone was erected in her memory. And though she lived on in the hearts of those who knew her, everyone who remembered her felt their own kind of pain. Berthe felt the debilitation of a parent whose child was taken from them too soon. Hilarion felt the heartbreak of a love that was never meant to be. And Albrecht? Albrecht felt the sharp pang of regret. The guilt of Giselle's death weighed on him heavily, and he resolved to visit her grave. On the very night that he chose to do so, Giselle was visited by none other than the Wilis. You see, Giselle's death and the circumstances that surrounded it had roused the Wilis' attention. In fact, it had roused the attention of their queen, Myrtha, and it was Myrtha who led the Wilis to Giselle's grave that one still night. Summoning Giselle's spirit from her grave, Myrtha enlisted Giselle as one of the Wilis. Giselle agreed and Myrtha led the Wilis into the forest in search of lonely wanderers, leaving Giselle at her graveside. It was then that Albrecht appeared by Giselle's gravestone. Overcome with emotion, his legs gave way beneath him and he wept uncontrollably. Oh, how selfish he had been when Giselle was alive! On witnessing this scene, Giselle chose to show her spirit to Albrecht. As soon as he saw her, he begged for forgiveness and Giselle, who had felt such anger up until that point, was able to see his remorse. Realizing that he had seen the error of his ways, Giselle decided to forgive Albrecht, and beseeched him to move on with his life. She left Albrecht at the spot of her grave and started her ghostly walk through the forest to meet her sisters, the Wilis. But little did she know that Albrecht was following her.

When Giselle at last found the Wilis, she was dismayed to see that they had Hilarion amongst them. The poor man had wandered into the woods to find Giselle's grave, but had taken a wrong turn and found himself surrounded by the wisps at the stroke of midnight. He had shouted out – begged them to spare him – but they compelled him to dance with them. This way and that he twisted, and his arms swept around him in an enchanted dance of which he had no control. Round and round he went with no way of stopping, until finally his body felt weak with exhaustion. Sensing that the end was nigh, the Wilis flung Hilarion into a nearby lake, letting his tired body sink eerily to the bottom.

It was not long before Giselle joined the Wilis, unaware of the terrible act they had recently committed. But on her arrival, she could see that, instead of welcoming her, the Wilis appeared to be interested in something – or someone – else. Someone who she could now see not far behind her. Albrecht! As the Wilis floated slowly towards him, Giselle cried out in fear. This was not what she wanted. Albrecht's mistake had cost her her life, but she did not want another person to die in vain. She had chosen to forgive him, and she didn't believe that he should die at the hands of the Wilis. Giselle stood between Albrecht and the Wilis to protect him, much to the anger of Myrtha. In an act of spite, the queen ordered Giselle to begin dancing and Giselle found herself unable to resist, such was the strength of the queen's magic. But to Giselle's horror, as she started to dance, so did Albrecht. Seeing the enchantment move his body filled Giselle with fear, for she knew he would not stop – he *could* not stop – now that she had compelled him.

In the hushed glade that night, Giselle and Albrecht danced together, and never before had even the Wilis seen such hauntingly beautiful dancing. But the revelry became faster and faster as other Wilis joined them. *Faster*, they seemed to say, *faster!* and Albrecht could not refuse.

Giselle watched him as the night wore on, and saw the tiredness creep into his limbs as the light in his eyes appeared to slowly extinguish. It was as if her heart was breaking once more. And as the brightness of dawn emerged from the horizon, and the Wilis abandoned the two dancing figures one by one, Giselle took one last look at her beloved before she too was pulled back to her grave. Knowing that this would be the last time she would ever see him, Giselle held out her hand as she fell back into the depths from which she had come. And as Albrecht reached out for her, he too fell. For after dancing with the Wilis, all that he wanted was to rest, and rest in peace he would.

The Wayward Daughter

"La Fille mal gardée", known in English as "The Wayward Daughter" is a comic ballet inspired by work of French artist Pierre-Antoine Baudouin. Originally choreographed by French dancer and ballet master Jean Dauberval, it premiered at the Grand Théâtre de Bordeaux, in Bordeaux, France, on 1st July 1789.

On a quiet but busy farm, there once lived a woman called Simone. Hard working but also poor, Simone wished the very best for her daughter Lise. Lise was a caring and kind young lady who was liked by all who knew her. In particular, she was liked by Colas, a young man whose heart she had been given, and to whom she in turn gave her own. However, love is a complicated thing, especially when mothers and fathers get involved, and Lise's mother was no exception to this rule. Simone knew that affection was held between her daughter and Colas, but she did not want that affection to grow. You see, Colas was poor. You might wonder what was so wrong about being poor, and the true answer to this is that there is in fact nothing wrong with being poor. But Simone had decided that, because she and Lise had lived so poorly for so long, she would not allow Lise to marry someone who was also poor themselves.

Because of this, Simone had set about joining her daughter with a suitor of her own choosing: a young man called Alain. The thought of marrying Alain filled Lise with dread – after all, she found him quite dull and rather silly. He certainly did not compare with her great love, Colas. However, Lise knew the real reason her mother wanted to match her with Alain. It was because of his wealth. And so, whenever Lise would try to sneak off to meet with Colas, her mother would prevent her from doing so and instead force her to spend time with the tedious Alain.

On one particularly warm autumn day,

when Lise and her mother were hard at work preparing for the harvest, Lise offered to leave the farm and work in the fields. But her mother said no. She realized that her daughter was once again attempting to steal away to meet Colas. To prevent her from doing so, Simone tasked Lise with working within the farmyard and told her not to leave the farm for any reason. Feeling sure that Colas would take it upon himself to come to her instead Lise set to work, and it wasn't long before her love did indeed arrive and hid himself behind the oil press. When Lise discovered him, they embraced lovingly, so pleased were they to see each other again. But their happiness was short-lived, as Simone – noticing that her daughter was no longer in the yard – quickly found them. Simone hurriedly shooed Colas away. She did not want this young man, who appeared to have no wealth to speak of, to capture her daughter's heart.

Soon enough, harvest time arrived, and the local villagers began harvesting crops. For many, this was a happy time, but of course it was not a happy time for Lise. On that particular day, there was a knock on the door of Lise and her mother's house, and when Lise opened the door she was surprised to see not only Alain but Alain's father, Thomas, standing before her. "We are all going for a picnic," declared Simone from inside the house, and though Lise tried her best to protest, her mother would not listen.

The four people began their picnic in the fields, though Lise was decidedly frosty with Alain, such was her irritation to be there. But before long they were joined by farm workers who were celebrating the harvest by taking part in a ribbon dance around the maypole. "You must dance together," urged Simone, though she knew that her daughter did not wish to do so. Upon seeing her resistance, Alain's father urged the same, and, feeling under much pressure, Lise succumbed to their demand and agreed to dance with Alain. However, just as they were about to, there started a rumble in the sky.

As they looked above them, the small party saw flashes of lightning in the distance and realized that a storm was coming. Indeed, judging by the sound of thunder in the distance, the storm would be upon them in no time at all. Quickly the picnic was packed up and the families bid each other goodbye. For Simone, Thomas and Alain the disruption was a frustrating one, but as Lise ran back to the farm with her mother she couldn't help smiling with joy, such was her relief that they had been interrupted.

Once home, Lise busied herself by spinning at the spinning wheel, and her mother decided to do the same as it allowed her to keep a watchful eye over her daughter. But soon there came knocks at their front door as the farm workers brought back the bales of hay they had salvaged from the rain. Knowing that she would need to lead them to the stables, Simone decided to lock Lise indoors to make sure that she would not run off to visit Colas.

Left alone indoors, Lise daydreamed of Colas. But suddenly she realized that she was not alone. There was someone in the room with her, and to her surprise, Lise saw that it was in fact Colas himself! "You must leave!" cried Lise, for although she wished to spend time with him, she knew that her mother would be furious if she found them together. But when Colas tried to go they found that

Simone had locked the front door, leaving them both trapped inside the house. Upon realizing that they had no choice but to remain inside, the two young loves became happy to spend time together. As a mark of their love for each other, they exchanged handkerchiefs, with Colas carefully placing his around Lise's neck. But suddenly they heard a noise at the door. Simone was back. Lise had only enough time to hide Colas in the larder and return to her spindle before her mother appeared in the room. But Lise had forgotten something: the handkerchief that remained tied around her neck. Upon seeing this, Simone knew that, somehow, Colas had been there, and, in her anger, she locked Lise in the larder, not realizing that she was inadvertently locking her daughter in a room with her beloved.

"I've had enough of your sneaky

behaviour!" called her mother through the door, but her shouting was interrupted by Alain, who had brought with him a wedding contract for Lise to sign. Simone felt overcome with relief upon seeing Alain, as she felt that this would be the moment when her daughter would finally marry him. But, when she stood Alain in front of the larder door and opened it, they were both surprised to find Lise and Colas locked in an embrace. You see, the two loves had feared that this would be their last moment together, so they had clung to each other dearly, not knowing what else to do. And it was while they were doing so that Simone had opened the door and revealed them.

When Alain saw Lise and Colas together, he flew into a rage and even ripped up the marriage contract. As he stormed out of the farmhouse, Lise and Colas fell to

Simone's feet and begged her forgiveness. "Please, mother," said Lise, "please let us be together. I love Colas so." Finally, Simone understood. Though she had wanted to make the best possible match for her daughter, nothing could get in the way of true love. And so it was that she gave her blessing to Lise and Colas, agreeing that they could marry.

The Nutcracker and the Mouse King

Originally written by German author ETA Hoffmann in 1816 and titled, "The Nutcracker and the Mouse King", the story of the Nutcracker was also revised by French writer Alexandre Dumas in 1844 and turned into a two-act ballet in 1892 – both of which were titled simply, "The Nutcracker". The ballet, which drew upon both Hoffmann and Dumas' writings, was created by Russian composer Pyotr Ilyich Tchaikovsky and Russian choreographers Marius Petipa and Lev Ivanov.

ON CHRISTMAS EVE

Oh, why did Christmas Eve feel like such a long day? For much of the twenty-fourth of December, the children of Doctor Stahlbaum were not permitted to enter the parlour, and they could certainly not go into the drawing room, such was the secrecy surrounding their Christmastime celebrations. Frederic and Maria sat in a darkened corner of their back chamber, feeling gloomy. When would they be allowed into the forbidden chambers? "I stopped outside the door this morning and heard a rustling noise and a rattling noise," said Fred in a quiet whisper. "I think I heard something *knock-knock*-ing too." He had also seen Godfather Drosselmeier walking almost silently through their front door with a large chest under his arm, or so he told his sister.

Maria clapped her hands together with joy. "I wonder what beautiful things Godfather Drosselmeier has made for us this time!" she exclaimed.

Godfather Drosselmeier was small and thin, with many wrinkles on his face. From time to time the children had wondered aloud what age he might be, but of course it was impossible to tell. "A hundred? Maybe even older," Fred had said once, much to Maria's shock. Over Godfather Drosselmeier's right eye rested a black patch, and his head had not one hair upon it, but he wore a white wig made entirely of glass. The wig really was an ingenious piece of work, and Godfather had made it himself. He was ingenious also, understanding all about clocks, mechanics and inventions as he did. He could even make them. When any one of the beautiful clocks in Doctor Stahlbaum's house stopped working, it was Godfather Drosselmeier who would fix it. Along he would come, with his bag of tools, and he would sit before the clock in question, lifting his glass wig and scratching his head beneath it as he mulled over what the problem might be. Soon enough, the clock would become quite lively again, and begin to strike and sing just as it had before.

Each Christmas Eve, Godfather Drosselmeier would bring something extra-special for the children – something grand that he had built himself – and now the children took to guessing what the gift might be this time. "It will surely be a castle," said Fred, "filled with fine soldiers there to protect it." But Maria disagreed. "Godfather Drosselmeier told me just last week of a beautiful garden where there is a great lake on which swans swim. The swans sing beautiful songs, and there is a girl who coaxes the swans to shore and feeds them cake. Surely he is making us a garden just like it!"

"Even Godfather Drosselmeier can't make a whole garden, silly!" said Fred, "and besides, swans don't eat cake." The children continued their game of guessing, each suggesting ideas that were put in question by the other. They did this for quite some time, so that darkness fell outside without them even realizing. Suddenly, the doors to the chamber flew open and such a dazzling light flooded through that the children's hands flew up to their faces to shield their eyes from it. As they did so, they felt their parents by their sides and heard them gently saying, "Come, come, dear children and see what Christmas has brought you this year."

THE GIFTS

Dear reader, or listener, whatever your name may be, I beg you to recall the very first time you saw Christmas presents in their many. Freshly wrapped and lying beneath a tree or upon a table, do you remember the excitement you felt upon seeing them? If you do, then you will also be able to imagine the astonishment that Fred and Maria both felt in that moment, as candles shone brightly around them. A fir tree stood in the middle of the room, and the decorations on it sparkled as the candlelight reflected upon them. As the children drew closer they saw that gold and silver apples, sugar almonds, comfits and lemon drops all hung from the branches like blossom in springtime. But the most beautiful thing about the tree was the many little lights that twinkled about its branches. They looked like stars in the night sky.

"Oh, how beautiful!" cried Maria, after a moment of stunned silence. She was certain that she had never seen a sight as splendid as this, despite Christmas coming every year. And such was Frederic's excitement that he leapt into the air higher than he ever had before. "You must have been extremely well-behaved children," said their father, "to deserve such gifts." Frederic looked to the table beneath the tree and saw a bay horse resting there, waiting for him. He took it up and rode about the room, calling out to his imaginary regiment of soldiers. Meanwhile, Maria spied a set of beautiful books, all written by her favourite authors. She touched their covers gently, feeling the embroidery beneath her fingers. She had never owned books like these before. Fred, momentarily tired of his horse, found that he too had books, and he set about looking through them, although he handled them somewhat more roughly than Maria had hers. In turn, Maria spotted a fine violin that was meant for her. Its deep red wood was almost mirror-like and felt smooth to touch. Just when the children felt as if nothing could be more exciting than what they were experiencing in that very moment, they heard a loud, *ring, ring, ring* and they gasped with delight. Godfather Drosselmeier was ready to unveil their present! He strode across the room, full of Christmas spirit and with a large smile upon his face, and the children cheered. Silently he led them to a table shrouded by a curtain that reached from the ceiling all the way to the floor. The children waited eagerly, but they did not have to wait long. Godfather Drosselmeier grasped a rope and – *whoosh!* – the curtain swung open.

What did the children see? Oh, it was a beautiful scene, for there stood a noble castle with clear glass windows and golden turrets. It stood upon a lush green meadow that was dotted with flowers of all colours, and upon the castle the children saw a clock. At once the clock began to play music and the castle's door and windows flew open to reveal little women and men in each of the rooms. In the castle's middle hall, there were chandeliers and children dancing to the sound of the music. At intervals, a tiny man in an emerald green cloak would pop his head out of one of the windows, only to nod and pop back out of sight. Why, even a small version of Godfather Drosselmeier himself was there in the castle, no taller than their father's thumb! Every now and then the little figure would move to the open door, look about, and go back inside again.

Fred, with his arms resting upon the table on which the castle stood, stared at the scene in wonder. "Oh, Godfather Drosselmeier, I wish I could go inside the castle," he said. But of course, this was quite impossible, for the castle, even with its golden turrets, was not as tall as he. Soon the children realized that each small person within the castle would always do the same thing. The children would always dance in the same way, the little men and women would always move in the same way within each room, and the little Godfather Drosselmeier would always come to the open door, look about, and then go back inside. "Can the man in the green cloak look out of another window instead?" asked Maria. "And can the children go outside to dance?" asked Fred. But Godfather Drosselmeier said that could not be. The castle was mechanical, and every character had its own set routine that could not be altered. "As the mechanism is made, so it must remain," said Godfather Drosselmeier.

THE FAVOURITE

After watching the castle for some time, the children started to lose interest and so looked to busy themselves with other toys. Fred darted off to play with the horse figurines that stood proudly in a row, but Maria walked close to the table as she had discovered something there, hidden between the boughs of the tree. At first she had not noticed the dear fellow – indeed, no one had – but somehow he had come into view, as if he had simply been waiting quietly for his turn. He wore a beautiful bright jacket that was fastened together with white loops and buttons, and beneath that Maria could see his pantaloons of exactly the same colour and the smartest boots that ever did grace the feet of an officer. As well as his smart clothes, the figure wore a wooden cloak upon his back and a woodman's cap upon his head. The longer Maria gazed at the little man, the more she took a liking to him and felt that she could see nothing but good nature and friendliness shown in his clear green and somewhat prominent eyes.

"Father," she asked, "who does this charming little man belong to? I found him in the tree."

"He belongs to you both," her father replied, "and shall work very hard indeed for everyone, as he is a nutcracker, my dear, and can crack nuts between his teeth." Her father took the nutcracker carefully from the tree and lifted his wooden cloak. As he did so, the nutcracker's mouth stretched open wide and revealed two rows of white teeth. Maria placed a nut within the nutcracker's mouth and – *crack* – the little man bit down on it and the shell cracked to reveal the sweet nut inside. *What a clever little nutcracker!* thought Maria. Her father, noticing that Maria was particularly fond of this gift, gave her responsibility of it. "Since our friend Nutcracker is your favourite," he said, "I place him under your particular care, although you must remember that he does belong to the rest of the family too."

This pleased Maria enormously, and she hugged dear Nutcracker. When she used him to break the nuts, she chose only the small ones so as not to stretch the poor fellow's mouth too wide. While this was happening, Frederic had become somewhat bored and now appeared by her side looking for amusement. He laughed heartily at the little man who could crack nuts with his teeth. "I want to use the nutcracker," he said to Maria, and though she was alarmed by the roughness with which Fred snatched Nutcracker away, she was reminded of her father telling her that he must be shared.

Fred set to at once, breaking nuts within the nutcracker's mouth. But instead of picking small nuts as Maria had done, Fred picked the largest nuts he could find. *Crack*, went the nuts. *Crack, crack, crack!* When suddenly there was a crack that sounded different to the others, and to her horror Maria saw three white teeth fall from Nutcracker's mouth. "Oh no!" cried Maria, and she snatched him from Fred's hands. "Oh, Fred, how could you?"

"How could I?" said Fred. "That silly

fellow wants to be a nutcracker but has poor teeth. Let's take all of the teeth out and use him all the same." Of course, Maria would not allow this and couldn't believe her brother's suggestion. They began to fight so loudly that their parents and Godfather Drosselmeier came over to see what the matter was. "Tell her she's being a baby!" said Fred, but their father put his hand on Fred's shoulder. "I placed Nutcracker under Maria's protection," he said, "and now I see that he is greatly in need of her care. So let's leave him with Maria and busy ourselves with the other things with which we have been gifted."

Knowing that his father disagreed with his behaviour made Fred feel rather ashamed, and without another word he went off to look for something else to play with. Maria collected together Nutcracker's lost teeth and tied up his wounded chin with a nice white ribbon that she had taken from her dress.

WONDERS UPON WONDERS

In the sitting room of Maria and Frederic's house stood a tall glass case in which they stored their many wonderful toys. Godfather Drosselmeier's clever inventions were always placed on the top shelf, their books were placed on the next shelf down, and the remaining two shelves were used however Maria and Fred wished, but Fred usually put his toys on the higher shelf and Maria usually put hers on the lower.

It was now very late and soon to be bedtime. Godfather Drosselmeier had long since gone home, and the children were tasked with arranging their toys within the glass case so that they could be kept safe for the night. Fred did so quickly and off he ran to bed, but Maria took time to arrange her toys and books nicely. As her mother blew out the last of the candles, she urged Maria to bed. "Please may I stay here a while longer," said Maria. "Just until I've finished this task." Knowing that Maria was a sensible child, her mother agreed, but only if Maria would not be long. Maria knew that she would not, for she had just one thing to do: looking after Nutcracker. As soon as her mother had gone, Maria set to it. She opened her doll's house and arranged the furniture within, then placed Nutcracker on one of the soft beds and examined his wound. "Poor Nutcracker," she sighed. "I will tend to you carefully until you are quite well again. And perhaps Godfather Drosselmeier will help me fasten your teeth again, as he is so good at these things." Upon saying Godfather Drosselmeier's name, Maria was shocked to observe Nutcracker's face change. It seemed as though his green eyes flashed somehow and at once it scared her, but not even a moment later Nutcracker's face was as it always had been and Maria told herself that it must have been the glow of the lamp that stood beside her that had made Nutcracker's face look different.

Maria closed the cabinet door and locked it tight, and was about to make her way upstairs when she heard a peculiar sound. It was a rustle at first, but then it sounded like a whisper, and a *rattle-rattle* that seemed to go round and round the room, underneath the chairs, behind the cupboards and over the glass cabinet. The great clock that stood in the corner started to whir, and the noise got louder and louder as the clock tried to strike but couldn't. There was a large gilt owl atop the clock, and Maria was sure that she saw it move. It seemed to stretch out its neck as the clock whirred and whirred until it sounded as if the clock was actually speaking.

Dickory, dickory, dock,
softly clock.
Mouse King has a fine ear,
the old song let him hear.
Or he might
run away in fright,
now, clock, strike softly and light.

Suddenly, *pum! Pum!* Went the clock, twelve whole times, the sound dull and ominous, and Maria began to tremble with fear. She started to run from the room, but thought she saw Godfather Drosselmeier standing at the top of the clock where the owl had been. "Godfather Drosselmeier," she cried, "come down from there, please! You're frightening me so!"

As Maria looked about her in panic, she started to hear a rumble of sound, as if a stampede of a thousand tiny feet was thundering towards her. Thousands of small lights revealed themselves, but they were not lights, Maria saw, they were eyes and they belonged to mice. They surrounded her as they swarmed into the room. Now that she could see the source of all this noise, Maria's fear started to leave her, for she was not afraid of mice. She watched the curious creatures running into the room and was amazed to see them line up in perfectly straight rows, as if they were soldiers from one of Fred's games.

Now I know, dear reader, that you are as brave as anyone can be, but I do believe that if you had seen what Maria was seeing, then you would have run away as quickly as you possibly could. And perhaps Maria would have done exactly that if not for the fact that, at that moment, the floor right beside her feet burst open and seven mice heads wearing seven crowns rose out of the floor, squeaking and squealing and squealing and squeaking — oh, the noise was awful! Soon enough, the mouse body to which the seven heads belonged also worked its way out and the enormous mouse, wearing the seven diadems and making such a racket, huzzaed in full chorus as he strode forward to meet his army.

Trot, trot, trot, trot, went the army, now in motion again and marching straight towards the glass cabinet, in front of which poor Maria was still standing.

This is probably a good time, dear reader,

for us to consider how Maria might have felt in this moment. Perhaps you are thinking back to a time when you felt particularly scared. Was your heart beating firmly in your chest? Was your skin prickling? Were the hairs on your arms standing on end? Poor Maria. So overcome with anxiety and fear was she that she felt as if her heart would burst out of her chest completely. *Thump-thump-thump-thump,* it went, and she stumbled backwards into the cabinet, falling against it so forcefully that she struck the glass pane with her elbow and it gave a loud *crack* as it shattered and fell to the floor in pieces.

Maria felt a sharp pain in her arm, but in that moment her heart also became much lighter, and the overwhelming noise – all the squeaking – suddenly became still. Maria realized that she had covered her eyes with her hands, but dared not uncover them for fear of what she would see. Had the mice run away, scared by the clatter of the broken glass? Close behind her in the cabinet, a rustling began once more, and Maria heard a series of fine voices ringing out.

Up, up, awake
arms take, awake
to the fight
this night,
up, up
to the fight.

As she heard the words, Maria was also aware of a sound – like beautiful chiming bells – ringing out loud and clear. "Oh, it must be the dear musical clock!" exclaimed Maria, and, feeling cheered, she joyfully turned to look. But the clock was sparking and flashing strangely within the cabinet, and the figures within it were moving around in the most peculiar fashion, stretching out their arms and legs as if preparing for something. And now, Maria saw, Nutcracker was moving too. Off he threw the cover that Maria had placed upon him and up he leapt from the bed on which he'd been lying. Leaping to both feet, he drew his little sword and waved it in the air. "Friends!" he cried. "We must drive the mouse back. Will you stand by me in this fight?" Without hesitation, three Scaramouches, a Harlequin, four chimney-sweepers, two guitar players and a drummer called out, "Yes, my lord! We will follow you into battle with fidelity and courage. To victory!"

The toys started jumping from the shelves, and such were their cotton exteriors and soft insides that it was easy for them. But

Nutcracker was made of wood, and jumping from the shelf would surely have shattered him. Maria heard her dearest doll Clara call out. "Do not jump, dear lord, for you are sick and wounded. Your brave soldiers assemble themselves for you, please, continue your rest." But Nutcracker, feeling a strong sense of duty, could not heed Clara's words. The kindness and love that Maria had shown him before he had come to life filled him with strength, and down he leapt from the cabinet, ready to battle. As soon as he did so, the ear-splitting squeaking began again and Maria saw that the terrible mice had concealed themselves beneath a large table in the corner of the room, and high above them towered the dreadful mouse with seven heads. *Goodness*, thought Maria, *what terrible thing will happen next?*

THE BATTLE

"Beat the march, Drummer!" shouted Nutcracker, and on his bidding the drummer skilfully beat upon his drum a steady marching roll. As the drumbeat grew louder, Maria saw the boxes that housed Fred's army burst open as soldier upon soldier marched out. Nutcracker ran up and down the line of soldiers that were forming, steadying the troops' nerves and speaking words of encouragement. There was a shrill whistle and the glass cabinet stirred once more as all of Maria and Fred's toys leapt to life and made their way down the shelves. A cannon was sounded, *BOOM*, and some of the mice suffered for it. "Onward!" shouted Nutcracker. "ONWARD!"

Sugar plums flew through the air in their dark mass and covered the mice with white powder – which created not a small amount of disorder – and caraway seeds were fired by a heavy battery mounted upon a footstool. *Pum*, they went, as they flew across the room. *Pum! Pum! Pum-pum-pum!* Though the toys fought admirably, the mice were still advancing and their numbers seemed endless. Maria kicked and pushed at them, and used her arms to shelter herself while she tried to keep track of the battlefield throughout the smoke and dust that emerged from the cannons. The squeaks of the mice and squeals of their Mouse King were accompanied by the mighty voice of the Nutcracker as he made his commands. His brave army, Maria now saw, was made up of the most unusual assortment of toys. Chinese emperors, gardeners, tigers, peacocks – even cupids firing their arrows. Despite their efforts, a gap appeared in the defence and the enemy rushed through. Nutcracker was now completely surrounded, Maria saw with fear. As his troops fell around him, Nutcracker saw that there was no one to help, and Maria rushed forward from her place of safety just as he was seized by two enemies. "No!" shouted Maria, as the Mouse King squealed in triumph. Maria used all of her strength to push through the mice – oh, how hard it was – and rushed straight at their king. The mice seemed to disperse, but Maria, feeling the pain in her arm more fiercely than before, sank down to the floor and saw blackness all around her.

THE SICKNESS

When Maria woke from her deep, death-like slumber, she found herself lying in her own bed. Shafts of sunlight streamed through the window, and beside her sat someone who at first she did not recognize but then saw to be Surgeon Wendelstern. "She is awake," he said softly, and with that Maria's mother and father rushed to her bedside. "Oh, Maria," said her mother, "we are so glad you're awake, child, but you were so very naughty indeed."

"Naughty?" asked Maria in confusion. "But it was not I who was naughty, mother, it was the mice and their Mice King. Please," she said, "tell me, is Nutcracker safe?" Maria's parents drew back in surprise. "What are these mumblings?" they said to one another. "Our poor daughter seems quite delirious."

"Maria," said her mother with caution, "dear child, you stayed up late to play with your toys and made quite a mess. When we found you in the room the following morning, you were surrounded by toys – both yours and Frederic's – and you had hurt your arm terribly. There was shattered glass all around where you lay on the floor."

"Oh, mother, father, there was a terrible battle," cried Maria, by now feeling quite distraught. "There were toys and mice, and poor Nutcracker was taken as prisoner. I must have fainted after that, for I don't remember what happened next." Maria's parents looked at each other worriedly, and Surgeon Wendelstern stepped forward. "Never mind about it now, child. The mice are gone and little Nutcracker stands safe and sound in the glass cabinet, so all is well once more." Though his words were encouraging, Maria could tell that he did not believe her. As she sank back into her bed, she caught only some of what the grown-ups were saying.

"… must have a fever," said Surgeon Wendelstern. "… needs lots of rest."

"… will make sure she stays in bed," said Maria's father, and she closed her eyes. At least she knew that Nutcracker had escaped and was safe in the cabinet.

Over the days that followed, Maria sometimes thought she could hear Nutcracker calling to her, asking her for help. But her arm was still wounded and she was still bedridden, so all that Maria could do for quite some time was lay still. One evening, when Maria had just finished reading a wonderful book about the history of Prince Fackardin, her door opened and Godfather Drosselmeier strode in, asking, "And how is the sick and wounded Maria after all this time?" As soon as Maria saw him in his large overcoat, the night of the battle came flooding back to her once more and she cried out. "Oh, Godfather, why did you sit upon the clock that night, when you knew that it frightened me so? Why did you not help me and poor Nutcracker?" Curiously, Godfather Drosselmeier made a very strange face at Maria and in an odd, monotonous tone said:

"Pendulum must whirr, whirr, whirr, this way, that way,
clock will strike, tired of ticking all the day.
Owl in swift flight
comes at dead of night.
Softly whirr, whirr, whirr, strike
kling-klang, strike klang-kling,
bing and bang and bang and bing, t'will scare away the Mouse King."

All the while Maria stared at Godfather Drosselmeier, for he appeared to look and sound quite unlike himself. His right arm jolted backward and forward stiffly, as if he were a puppet pulled by strings, and Maria would have called out in fear had her mother not then walked through the door to check that she was all right. Frederic ran in alongside her and interrupted Father Drosselmeier's speech. "Haha, Father Drosselmeier, you look just like my Harlequin that I played with this morning." But their mother, seeing that Father Drosselmeier was acting peculiarly, was quite concerned. "Dear Counsellor," she said, "are you quite all right?"

As if in answer, Father Drosselmeier pulled up a chair next to Maria's bedside and drew something from his pocket. It was Nutcracker! His lost teeth were nicely fastened and he looked well again. Maria's mother smiled. "Now you see, Maria, that

Godfather Drosselmeier has no ill will towards your little Nutcracker." Before Maria could answer, Godfather Drosselmeier asked Maria if she had heard the story of Princess Pirlipat, the Lady Mouserings and the skilful Watchmaker. When Maria said she had not, Godfather Drosselmeier showed such surprise that both Maria and Frederic were eager to hear the tale. "Begin the story, dear Godfather!" they cried, and so the Counsellor began.

THE STORY OF THE HARD NUT

"The moment Princess Pirlipat was born, her parents were filled with joy. 'Never has a lovelier child been born!' exclaimed her father the king. Her cheeks were round, her eyes seemed to sparkle and her hair curled sweetly. It must be said, however, that there was something highly unusual about Princess Pirlipat: that she was born with two full rows of pearly white teeth. Indeed, but two hours after her birth she bit the high chancellor's finger as he cooed at her sweetly, causing him to cry out in pain. But I digress. As I said, the king and queen were delighted with their child. It was observed, however, that the queen was particularly anxious and uneasy after Princess Pirlipat's birth. Many people remarked with surprise the particular care with which she watched over her daughter's cradle, and the fact that the doors to Princess Pirlipat's room were guarded by soldiers. In addition to this, nurses would always be stationed close to the baby's cradle and six maids sat in the room to watch over the baby every night. But, however strange you believe all of this to be, it is not the strangest thing, for the queen had also ordered that each of the six maids must keep a cat upon their lap and pet it so that it purred constantly. Well, dear children, I feel it would be impossible for you to guess just why the queen insisted on all of this, so I will not make you try. Instead, I will simply tell you.

"It happened that, many years before, the king and queen were preparing for a royal banquet. While the food was being prepared in the royal kitchen, the queen made an appearance, as she knew that there was a particular dish that her husband so liked, and as a gift she wanted to make it for him herself. As she started to prepare her ingredients, she heard a small voice behind her, saying, 'Please, sister, allow me some food.' Upon hearing the voice, the queen immediately knew who it belonged to: it was Lady Mouserings. Lady Mouserings –

who was, as I am sure you have guessed, a mouse – had lived within the palace for many years. She insisted that she was related to the royal family and that she was a queen herself, who ruled over the kingdom of Mousalia.

"Now, Queen Pirlipat was a kind and benevolent woman, and although she did not believe that Lady Mouserings was actually a queen herself, she did not want to treat her unkindly. So in response to Lady Mouserings request, the queen said that she may help herself to one plate of food. Upon this, Lady Mouserings jumped straight up on to the tabletop and seized the food with her dainty little paws. The queen thought that Lady Mouserings would eat up and be gone, but no sooner had the mouse taken her first bite but did her seven sons – who were rather rude

and thoughtless mice, all seven of them –
reveal themselves and start feasting on the
food. When they had finished with one
plate, they simply moved on to another,
and as the queen watched with horror,
all of the food disappeared, leaving none
whatsoever for the royal banquet. As you
can imagine, the king and queen were
much displeased with this series of events,
and the queen was forced to admit that it
was Lady Mouserings and her seven sons
that had caused all the trouble. At once
the king resolved to take vengeance upon
Lady Mouserings, and a meeting was called.
Much discussion took place, but in the end
it was decided that the royal watchmaker
and mechanist would devise a series of traps
in which to imprison Lady Mouserings
and each of her sons.

"This man, who by coincidence bore

the same name as me – Christian Elias Drosselmeier – therefore invented a series of curious little machines inside of which a piece of delicious food was placed to entice the mice. Lady Mouserings was of course far too wise to be lured into the traps, but the same could not be said for her seven sons and, one by one, they succumbed to the traps and perished along with every other one of their mouse relatives. Distraught and forsaken, Lady Mouserings vowed to leave the palace, so filled with grief and despair was she. But before she did, she took great care to speak with the queen one last time. 'My sons, cousins, aunts and uncles have been destroyed,' she said with anger, 'and so I say this to you, queen: take care. Take care that I, the mouse queen, do not decide to turn on your daughter as you turned on my sons.' With that, Lady Mouserings left the palace.

"Upon her exit, the court revelled in joy but the queen was filled with deep concern. They had taken Lady Mouserings' seven sons from her, and the queen felt in her heart that revenge would indeed be sought."

"This truly is a grisly story, Godfather Drosselmeier," said Frederic with glee, and their mother was inclined to agree, worried as she was that the tale would scare her children. But both Fred and Maria were extremely curious to discover how the story ended, and though it was now very late and time for them to go to bed, they begged Godfather Drosselmeier to return the next day so that he might finish what he had started.

THE STORY OF
THE HARD NUT CONTINUED

When Godfather Drosselmeier once again took seat at the end of Maria's bed the following day, both children fell silent immediately, such was their eagerness for him to continue. And so he did.

"Now you must see quite clearly why Queen Pirlipat had been so scared for her daughter's safety. The watchmaker Drosselmeier's traps and machines were no match for Lady Mouserings, and the queen knew this as plain as day. For exactly this reason she had protected her daughter with the guards and the maids and the nurses and the cats. But would all of her precautions work? I think that perhaps you know the answer to this question, deep down. Late one night, one of the two chief nurses who sat next to the princess's cradle with a start from a deep sleep. The palace was silent and all around her the nurse felt such stillness, and with shock she realized that there was no sound of purring, or any sound at all. And that was not all. As the nurse looked about the room, she saw a dreadful, large mouse standing up on its hind legs so that it could see into the princess's cradle. So close was its horrible face to that of the princess that the nurse feared the oversized mouse would bite the princess. She called out in terror, waking everyone in close proximity. But her cry also alerted Lady Mouserings (for the great mouse was of course she) to the fact that she had been spotted. At once she ran as fast as she could to the far corner of the room and disappeared through a hole in the floor. Little Princess Pirlipat awoke from all the commotion and started to cry in the most alarming way, but, 'Thank goodness!' said the nurse with relief, 'she lives. She lives!' She then went to pick up the child to comfort her. But not in your darkest nightmares could you imagine the change that she saw when she looked into the princess's cradle. As if by some sorcery, the child's appearance had been dramatically altered: her head was now unnaturally large, with exaggerated features and an odd expression fixed upon her face. In contrast, her body had become very small and stiff. The king and queen were devastated. But not for one moment did they think to blame themselves for this terrible retaliation. Instead, they put the blame solely on Lady Mouserings. As it was the watchmaker Drosselmeier who had created the traps that caught Lady Mouserings' sons, so it was also the watchmaker Drosselmeier who the king now tasked with the duty of restoring Princess Pirlipat to her former self.

"Drosselmeier was more than a little terrified at this prospect, for what did he know of magic and such things? But with no choice in the matter, he set about trying to help the princess. He monitored her day and night, taking notes of her behaviour and habits. With great interest he noticed that, since the fateful night of Lady Mousering's visit, the princess had refused to do anything other than crack nuts. When confronted by this observation, the queen broke down and admitted something to Drosselmeier: immediately after her transformation, the princess had been inconsolable and nothing would stop her screaming. But when she noticed one of her nurses holding a nut, she immediately grabbed it from them and put it in her mouth, cracking it at once with her teeth and then eating the kernel.

From that point onwards the princess was quite composed, as long as she was kept in constant supply of nuts.

"On hearing this, Drosselmeier believed that he knew of the magic that had been used against the princess, and he also knew how to break it; although, to the king and queen's despair, Drosselmeier admitted that this would not be an easy task. As they stood before him in disbelieving silence, he explained the cure to them.

"'My king and queen,' he said, 'I have indeed heard of such magic as this and the cure is as strange as it is complicated. First, we must obtain a most rare type of nut, called Crackatuck. It has an exceptionally hard shell that has never been broken, but break it someone must if we are to have any hope of restoring the dear princess. It must be broken by a young man, cracked between his teeth, and then, while his eyes are shut, he must hand the princess the kernel found inside before marching seven steps backwards. If he fails to do any of these things, or if any elements are not exactly as I have just described, the restoration will not take place.'

"Seeing the challenge that lay ahead of them, the king and queen felt much sadness, but vowed to do all they could to help their daughter."

CONCLUSION OF
THE STORY OF THE HARD NUT

The next evening, as soon as candles had been lit to ward off the growing dark of night, Godfather Drosselmeier appeared and the children settled into silence so that he may continue his story.

"It took the watchmaker Drosselmeier

many years to find a Crackatuck nut," he began, "and even longer for him to find a boy capable of cracking it. But, as these things so often happen, the two events happened almost at the same time, for after fifteen years, when Drosselmeier was travelling with his faithful friend, an astrologer, a series of events led them directly to the exact nut they had been seeking for so long. That evening, while celebrating the find, Drosselmeier's astrologer friend was struck by an idea. "Good fortune rarely comes lonely," he exclaimed, and he went on to say that he believed Drosselmeier's brother's son – known as young Drosselmeier – to be the boy they had been looking for. It now occurred to Drosselmeier that his brother's son had become a handsome and well grown young man who was of exactly the same age as the princess. Thinking back to the last time he set eyes on him, Drosselmeier remembered the boy at Christmastime, when he would wear a handsome red coat trimmed with gold, with a hat under his arm and would carry a sword. In this fine dress, the boy would stand in his father's shop and crack nuts for customers. For this reason, he began to be known as the handsome Nutcracker.

"Very quickly it was arranged for the boy to visit the palace to perform his duty, and after young Drosselmeier had gracefully saluted the king, queen and princess, he was carefully handed the Crackatuck nut by the master of ceremonies. Without hesitation, Young Drosselmeier put the nut between his teeth and bit down as hard as he could. There was an almighty *CRACK-CRACK-CRACK* as the shell broke into many pieces. He then removed the kernel from inside, and with a low bow held it out for the princess, all the while closing his eyes. The princess took the kernel and swallowed it quickly, and — behold! — she changed again as the magic left her. Drums were beaten and trumpets were blown, and the celebrations immediately began. But poor young Drosselmeier — he had yet to take his seven steps backward. Much distracted by the joyous noise, he started to slowly step backwards, but as his leg stretched back on the seventh step he felt something beneath it and a loud squeak came from the floor. It was Lady Mouserings, who had made to distract him but had accidentally run directly beneath young Drosselmeier's foot. Down came his foot upon her head, and he stumbled in surprise as he tried to regain his balance. Falling to the floor, the young man was not able to complete his seventh step. Instead, he became cursed by the magic that had only moments before plagued the princess. His head became large, his green eyes stared out ahead and his mouth became ever so large and cumbersome. The cloak he wore upon his back became stiff and straight.

"The watchmaker felt numb with terror as he watched the scene unfold. Lady Mouserings lay on the floor nearby, severely hurt from being stood upon. Such were her injuries that it appeared she would not live for much longer. With her dying breath, the mouse queen spoke a curious riddle and everyone listened:

"Son with seven crowns will bite,
Nutcracker – at night, at night.
And revenge his mother's death –
short breath, short breath."

"With her final word, Lady Mouserings

perished, and was carried from the palace. But, dear children, you may be wondering what happened to Nutcracker. Is this so? The princess, so disgusted by him was she, asked for him to be removed from the palace immediately, and, beyond that day, few people troubled themselves to think any more about him. However, there was a rumour, though it was believed to be purely hearsay, that a prophecy said that young Drosselmeier would yet become a prince and king after the son of Lady Mouserings, who had been born with seven heads, was slain. This, children, is the story of the Hard Nut," concluded Godfather Drosselmeier

THE UNCLE AND NEPHEW

If any of you, dear readers, have ever had the misfortune of accidentally cutting yourself then you know how terribly it hurts, and for how long. And so it was for Maria. Whenever she tried to get up she was overcome by dizziness and this continued for a whole week, during which she had no choice but to stay in bed. But at last Maria became well again and could play around the house just as she had before. Everything was neat and tidy within the glass cabinet, she saw – all the books and toys. But, best of all, Nutcracker was there. He stood upon the second shelf and smiled at her with his good–as–new set of teeth, and Maria smiled back. But in the midst of her feeling this sense of happiness, a pang went through her heart, for she knew that Godfather Drosselmeier's story had not been a story at all but the truth about Nutcracker and how he had become himself. Her dear Nutcracker was the young Drosselmeier of Nuremburg – Godfather Drosselmeier's own nephew, enchanted by the terrible mouse queen, Lady Mouserings. And the skilful watchmaker who helped King and Queen Pirlipat so, well, it was the Counsellor Drosselmeier himself, and Maria had not doubted all of this for an instant since Godfather Drosselmeier had told them the whole story. "But why is it that your uncle hasn't helped you?" Maria asked Nutcracker aloud. "You are not able to move or talk to me, dear Master Drosselmeier, but still I know well enough that you understand me and know that I am a good friend to you. You may depend upon my help and I will beg your uncle to bring his skill and assistance to you whenever you have need of it." Nutcracker remained still and motionless, but Maria was certain that she felt a gentle sigh and saw the glass panes of the cabinet tremble slightly.

That evening at twilight, Maria heard her

father enter the sitting room with Godfather Drosselmeier. As the family engaged in conversation, Maria was sure to sit next to the Counsellor, and during a moment when they were all silent she took the chance to speak to him. "I know, dear Godfather, that my Nutcracker is your young nephew, Drosselmeier of Nuremburg. I understand the story you told and how it has all turned out. But why have you not helped him?" Maria started once more to recount the battle she had witnessed, but was interrupted by Frederic. "That story is not true – Mother told me it was your imagination and the fever," he said. But Godfather Drosselmeier looked at Maria with a strange smile and spoke to her more tenderly than he had ever spoken to her before, saying, "Ah, dear Maria, more power is given to you than me or any of the rest. You, like Pirlipat, are a princess, for you reign in a bright and beautiful kingdom. But you have much to suffer if you wish to fight for the poor misshapen Nutcracker, for the Mouse King watches him at every turn. I cannot rescue him. That is the destiny of you alone."

Neither Maria nor anyone else knew exactly what Drosselmeier meant by these words, but Maria's father was so taken aback that he felt the Counsellor's pulse and asked if he was feeling unwell. However, Maria's mother shook her head thoughtfully. "I feel that I somehow know what it is that the Counsellor means," she said, "but I cannot put it into words."

THE VICTORY

Not long after, Maria was woken one moonlit night by a strange scurrying that seemed to come from one corner of the chamber. Every now and then there was a terrible squeaking noise. "The mice are coming again!" said Maria in fright, and she tried to shout but her voice failed her. Frozen to the spot with fear, she saw the Mouse King work his way out of a hole in the wall. Up to her he ran, with his sparkling eyes and seven crowns, and with a desperate leap he sprang upon the little table that stood beside her bed. "Give me your books and your toys and your things, or I will bite thy Nutcracker!" he squeaked as he snapped and grated his teeth in the most hideous fashion. Then down he sprang and off he ran, pushing himself back through the small hole. Maria was so distressed that she was unable to sleep for the rest of the night, and the sight of her looking so tired and frightened truly alarmed her parents in the morning. A hundred times she thought to tell her mother and father of Fred and what had happened, but she stopped herself. After all, she knew that they wouldn't believe her. But this much was clear: if she wished to save the Nutcracker then she would need to give up her belongings to the Mouse King. Though the thought of this made her sad, Maria knew that she would give anything to help the Nutcracker. But also, she knew that if she gave in to the Mouse King's every demand, he would never stop making them. He would take and take and take until she had nothing to give, and surely then he would simply come for her.

As soon as she was alone in the sitting room, Maria stepped up to the glass cabinet. With tears in her eyes she looked at the Nutcracker. "What should I do?" she asked, though she knew he could not reply. It was in this moment that Maria observed a small spot of blood that had remained on the Nutcracker ever since the battle. Now, after Maria had realized that Nutcracker was actually young Drosselmeier, the Counsellor's nephew, she had stopped carrying him in her arms as she had before. Indeed, she would seldom touch or move him, as it did not feel appropriate. But when she saw the spot of blood, she took him carefully from the shelf on which he was standing and rubbed away the blood with her handkerchief. To her astonishment, as she did so, the Nutcracker began to move! Quickly she put him back upon the shelf again, and in amazement she saw his mouth begin to move. With a great deal of effort, he spoke at last, saying, "Dearest Miss Stahlbaum, excellent friend, however can I thank you for all that you have done? But I know. Please, get me a sword. A sword!" At that moment, speech left him once more and his eyes, which had only a moment ago expressed energy and life, became staring and motionless once more.

Through all of this, Maria had felt no fear – on the contrary, now she knew how she could help Nutcracker, and at once she went to find a sword. This was not a difficult task, as Fred had many for his toys, and without further ado Maria buckled a silver sabre about the Nutcracker so that he was armed once more.

That night, she could scarcely sleep, for she was so anxious and fearful. *Oh dear Nutcracker,* she thought, *please be safe!* At about midnight, she heard a noise outside her door and was struck with terror. "The Mouse King!" she cried as she sprang out of her bed. But presently she heard a gentle knocking at her door and a soft voice that said, "Worthiest Miss Stahlbaum, open the door without fear.

I have good tidings!" It was the Nutcracker! Maria recognized his voice at once, and she opened the door without hesitation. There little Nutcracker stood, with a bloody sword in his right hand. As soon as he saw Maria, he bent down upon one knee. "Dear lady," he said, "it was you who filled me with the courage and strength I needed to face the foe who dared disturb your slumber. The treacherous Mouse King is overcome and lies in a pool of his own blood." With these words, the Nutcracker took off the seven crowns of the Mouse King, which he had hung upon his left arm, and gave them to Maria, who received them with great joy. Nutcracker then arose. "There is so much I wish to show you, now that my enemy is gone," he said. "Oh, but will you follow me but a few steps, Miss Stahlbaum?"

THE PUPPET KINGDOM

I believe that all of you, dear children, would have agreed in an instant to follow the good, honest Nutcracker, for he could never be evil. And so Maria agreed to go with him. "But it must not be far," she said, "and I cannot stay long." The Nutcracker nodded and led Maria to a large antique wardrobe that stood in the hall. To her astonishment, the doors, which were usually always kept locked, now stood wide open and she could see within it her father's large travelling coat. Nutcracker pulled upon a tassel, and immediately a set of stairs appeared from the sleeve. "Ascend, if you please," said the Nutcracker, and Maria did so. Scarcely had she climbed up the sleeve when she was surrounded by a million tiny sparks of light which darted about like flashing jewels. As she looked about her, she saw that they were now standing in a sweet-smelling meadow. The Nutcracker held his arms open wide. "This is candy meadow," he said, and he led her through a gate – from a distance it looked to be white, brown and raisin-coloured, but as she neared it Maria saw that the whole thing was made of sugar, almonds and chocolate, all baked together. Very soon Maria smelt the sweetest fragrance. The smell became stronger as they came to a wood, with golden and silvery fruit hanging from trees. "Oh, how delightful it is here!" exclaimed Maria, as Nutcracker told her that the place in which they were standing was called Christmas Wood.

They walked alongside Orange Brook, which babbled and frothed and created a perfume so beautiful in scent that Maria gasped. But that did not compare to Lemonade River, which rustled and dashed, rolling around in the most glorious lemon-coloured billows. Nutcracker showed Maria Gingerbreadville and Treacle river, where pretty but ill-tempered people lived. "They suffer a good deal from toothache," explained Nutcracker, so we will not get too close." Through Bonbon Town they walked, until they came to a glorious lake filled with beautiful swans. At once Maria recognized it as the lake Godfather Drosselmeier had told her so much about, "He said he would make this lake for me," she told Nutcracker. But Nutcracker laughed bitterly, such as Maria had never seen of him before. "Godfather Drosselmeier could never make anything like this," he said. "But let us sail across Rose Lake to the capital."

THE CAPITAL

Nutcracker clapped his hands together, and Maria saw a boat of shells emerge from the lake. Over the lake they sailed, with the rosy air rushing around them, and they soon reached the other side where they were greeted by a thicket even more beautiful and sweet-smelling than Christmas Wood. "This is Cake Grove," said Nutcracker, "but just over there is the Capital." Maria looked in the direction in which Nutcracker was pointing, and, oh! What a sight! How can I begin to describe, dear reader, the beauty and splendour of the city that now stood before them. Not only did the walls and towers glitter in the brightest of colours, but the styles of the buildings were unlike anything Maria had ever seen before in her own world. Nutcracker was warmly welcomed by everyone they saw, and a beautiful Sugar Plum Fairy danced in celebration of their arrival. Maria noted with slight surprise that they all called Nutcracker "Prince". "Please, dear Nutcracker," she said after a moment, "tell me: what is this wonderful place."

"It's called Confectionville," said Nutcracker, "and it is a truly merry city. Let us walk awhile." Confectionville was filled with all sorts of people – people who had come here from many different places but who lived here together harmoniously. All of them welcomed Maria with such grace and kindness that she almost felt at home in this unusual and exciting place. When one of Nutcracker's subjects asked him to relay an account of his terrible battle with the Mouse King, he began his narration as Maria stood next to him, and as he did so Maria became aware of his voice growing more and more distant, until finally she could scarcely hear it. A light appeared before her and she walked towards it with the feeling that she was being lifted up and up, higher and higher.

THE CONCLUSION

When Maria next opened her eyes, she found herself lying upon her bed. It was bright as day and, looking up, she saw her mother before her. "How is it that you have slept so long, child?" she asked. "Breakfast has been ready a great while, and we are all downstairs waiting for you." As you may guess, dear reader, Maria had been so overcome by excitement that she had fallen asleep while in Confectionville and been carried safely home. Though she awoke in her own bed, she did not for a second doubt that her visit to another land had actually taken place. Over the breakfast table she told her family of the wondrous things she had seen, but in return they were quite disbelieving. "You had a long and beautiful dream," said her mother, "but now you must shake it from your head entirely." At this moment, Godfather Drosselmeier arrived and Maria felt sure that he would believe her, but this was not to be. The Counsellor's face grew dark and grave, and Maria felt she had angered him by speaking of such things. And so Maria realized that she would no longer be able to speak of the other world she had visited, or the Nutcracker and the adventure they had shared. With sadness, she sat close to the glass cabinet and, wondering aloud, she looked to the Nutcracker and said, "Oh, dear Master Drosselmeier, if only you were living. I would not reject you like Princess Pirlipat. I would not slight you because of your changed appearance. I would accept you for who you are."

Suddenly a noise from behind Maria startled her so, and she span around to see her mother. "Maria," she said happily, "we have a visitor. Here is Godfather Drosselmeier's nephew, just arrived from Nuremberg! Come now, do say hello." Looking up, Maria saw a young man wearing a handsome coat trimmed with gold. As he approached her, he stopped first at a small table on which a bowl of nuts stood. Picking one up, he held it before her and smiled, and then cracked it with his teeth. As he held out the kernel to her, Maria accepted the gift from this young man who she already knew but had only just met, and smiled back at him affectionately.

Now discover another selection of enchanting tales...

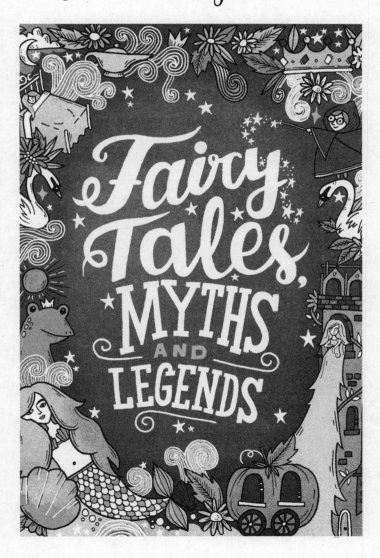